Jingle Bells

Written by Diane Muldrow
Illustrated by Joe Ewers

D1443709

 A GOLDEN BOOK • NEW YORK

Golden Books Publishing Company, Inc., New York, New York 10106

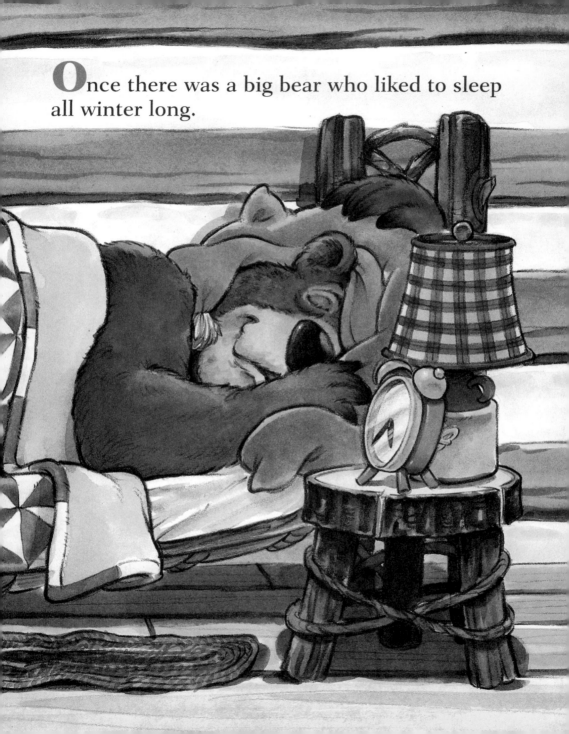

Once there was a big bear who liked to sleep all winter long.

One snowy day the bear was awakened by lots
of noises: *Clip-clop, clip-clop! Jingle, jingle, jangle!*

The bear covered his head with his pillow—
but the noises got louder and louder: *Jingle,
jingle, jangle!* Ha-ha-ha-ha-ha!

"Blast those jangly jingle bells!" shouted the
bear. He threw back the covers and marched
outside.

There, in the snow, were horses pulling
sleighs full of happy, noisy animal friends.

"Stop making all that racket!" said the bear.

"We were just about to stop—for some hot cocoa," said a rabbit. "Would you like some?"

The bear did not want to make friends with the rabbit, but the cocoa smelled so warm and chocolaty that he took a cup—and drank it all up!

"Delicious!" said the bear, who was starting to feel not so grumpy. "Er—where is everyone going?"

"Over the fields! Through the woods!" said the rabbit. "Climb in!"

"Here we go!" everyone shouted as they felt the pull of the sleigh. The horses began to trot—*clip-clop, clip-clop*—faster and faster until their sleigh bells went *jingle, jingle!*

"Whee!" cried the bear as the cold air hit his furry face. "This is fun!"

Off through the snow rode the happy group,
singing loudly. And this is what they sang:

"Dashing through the snow in a one-horse open sleigh,

"O'er the fields we go, laughing all the way!

"Bells on Bobtail ring, making spirits bright,

"What fun it is to ride and sing a sleighing song tonight!

"Jingle bells! Jingle bells! Jingle all the way! Oh, what fun it is to ride in a one-horse open sleigh!

"Jingle bells! Jingle bells! Jingle all the way!
Oh, what fun it is to ride in a one-horse open
sleigh! HEY!"

The bear felt cozy inside as he rode along
on the sparkling snow with his new friends,
listening to the sound of those jingly, jangly,
jolly jingle bells.

Jingle Bells

Brightly

Dash - ing through the snow, In a one - horse o - pen sleigh,

O'er the fields we go, Laugh - ing all the way;

Bells on bob - tail ring, Mak - ing spir - its bright; What

fun it is to ride and sing A sleigh - ing song to - night!

Jin - gle bells! Jin - gle bells! Jin - gle all the way!

Oh what fun it is to ride In a one - horse o - pen sleigh, Oh

Jin - gle bells! Jin - gle bells! Jin - gle all the way!

Oh what fun it is to ride In a one - horse o - pen sleigh! Hey!